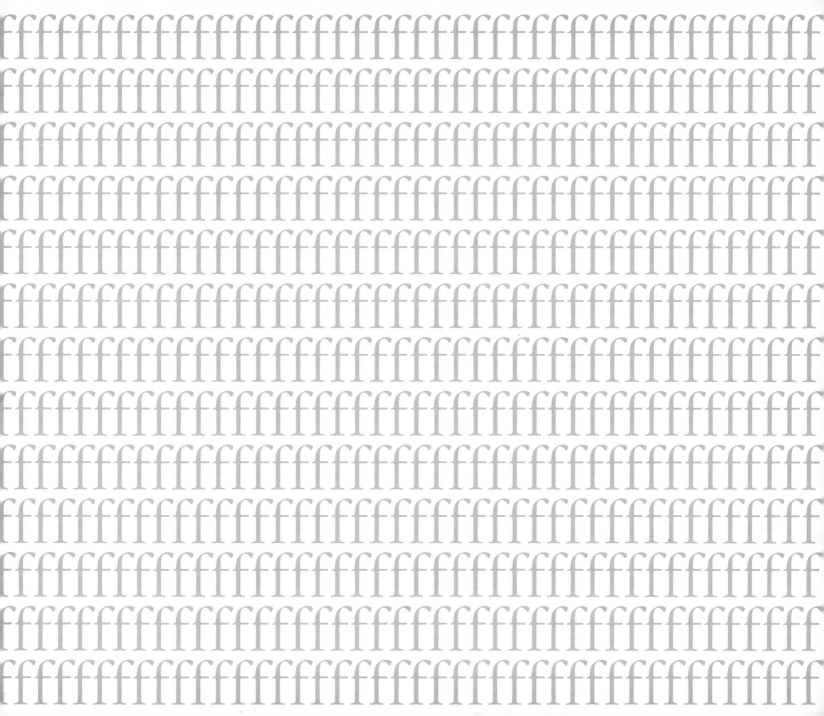

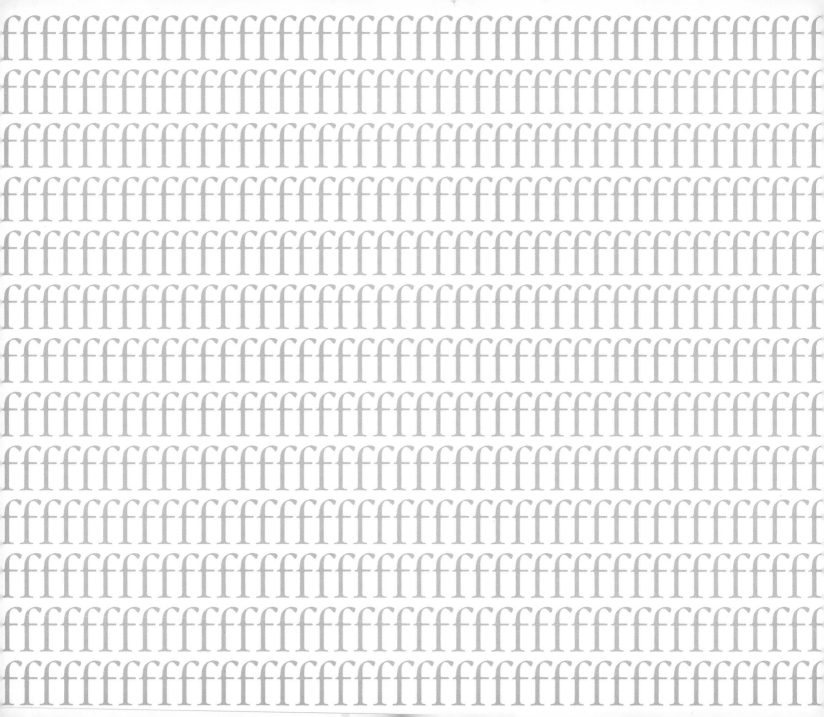

My "f" Sound Box®

(Blends are included in this book.)

Library of Congress Cataloging-in-Publication Data
Moncure, Jane Belk.
My "f" sound box / by Jane Belk Moncure; illustrated by Colin King.
p. cm.
Summary: A little girl fills her sound box with many words beginning with the letter "f."
ISBN 1-56766-772-4 (lib. reinforced : alk. paper)
[1. Alphabet.] I. King, Colin, ill. II. Title.
PZ7.M739 Myf 2000
[E]—dc21   99-056562

My "f"
Sound Box®

Jane Belk Moncure

illustrated by Colin King

The Child's World®

Little  had a box.

"I will find things that begin with my 'f' sound," she said.

"I will put them into

my sound  box."

Little  found a fishing pole.

She caught
four fish.

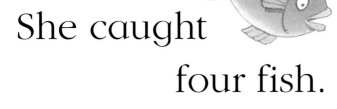

Did she put the
fishing pole and the
four fish into her box?

She did.

Then she caught five fat frogs.

Did she put the five fat frogs into the box with the fishing pole and the four fish? She did.

Little  walked through a forest of fir trees.

She put a fir tree into her box.

"I will leave the other fir trees in the forest," she said.

Suddenly, she saw a 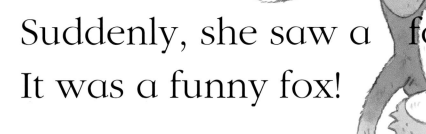 fox.
It was a funny fox!

"I will put this funny fox
into my box," said Little  f.

"What funny things I have in my box!
I have a fishing pole,
four fish, five frogs,
a fir tree, and a fox!"

Little  came to a fence.

She climbed over the fence and saw . . .

a field of flowers.

Little 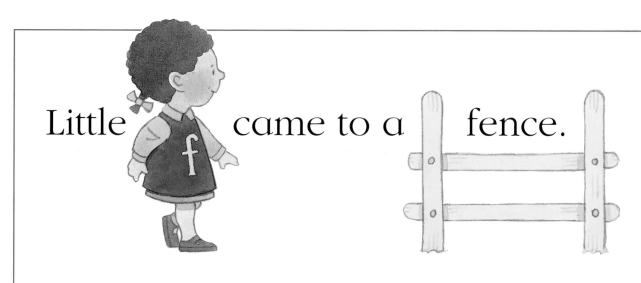 came to a fence.

She climbed over the fence and saw . . .

a field of flowers.

She filled her box with flowers.

Then Little  f saw a farmhouse.

The farmer ran from the farmhouse.

"Fire!" he cried.
"The farmhouse is on fire! Help!"

"Fire! Fire!" cried Little  f.

She ran back through the field of flowers,

over the fence,

through the fir forest,

and all the way to the . . .

19

fire station.

"Fire! Fire! Fire!" she shouted.
"The farmhouse is on fire!"

She rang the fire alarm.

Five firefighters jumped on
a fire engine.

Little  jumped on, too.

They gave Little  a fire hose,

a firefighter's hat,

boots,

and a firefighter's coat.

The fire engines went fast.

The firefighters put out the fire.

"Thank you," said the farmer.

"Thank Little  f ,"

said the five firefighters.

"She is our friend."

Then the firefighters took Little f and her box back to the fire station.

Little  opened her box and took out the funny fox.

They played
with all her things.

fishing pole

four fish

My! What fun they had!

five fat frogs

flowers

fox

fir tree

27

Can you read these words with Little f ?

feet

fan

fork

flute

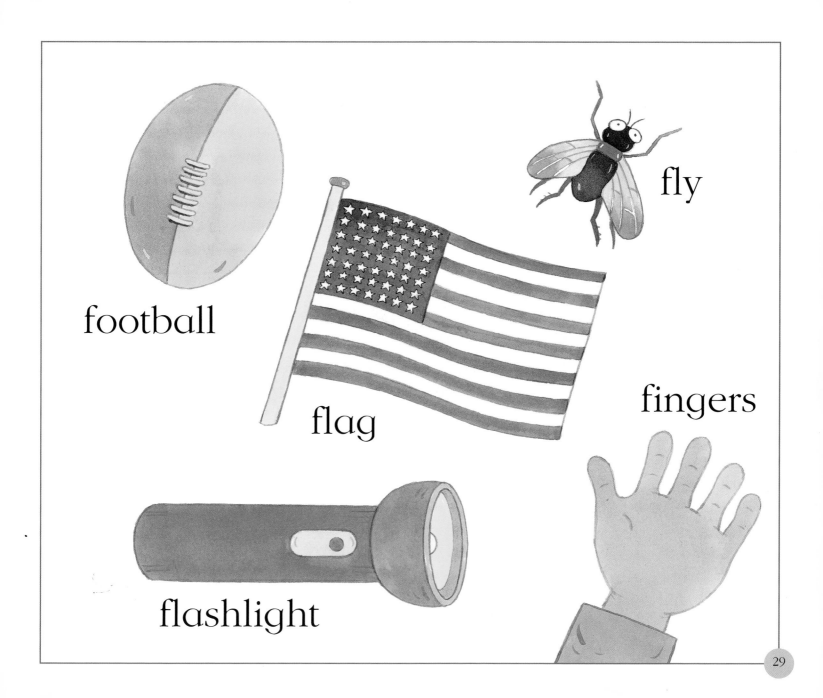

football

flag

fly

fingers

flashlight

29

ABOUT THE AUTHOR AND ILLUSTRATOR

Jane Belk Moncure began her writing career when she was in kindergarten. She has never stopped writing. Many of her children's stories and poems have been published, to the delight of young readers, including her son Jim, whose childhood experiences found their way into many of her books.

Mrs. Moncure's writing is based upon an active career in early childhood education.
A recipient of an M.A. degree from Columbia University, Mrs. Moncure has taught and directed nursery, kindergarten, and primary grade programs in California, New York, Virginia, and North Carolina. As a former member of the faculties of Virginia Commonwealth University and the University of Richmond, she taught prospective teachers in early childhood education.

Mrs. Moncure has travelled extensively abroad, studying early childhood programs in the United Kingdom, The Netherlands, and Switzerland. She was the first president of the Virginia Association for Early Childhood Education and received its award for outstanding service to young children.

A resident of North Carolina, Mrs. Moncure is currently a full-time writer and educational consultant. She is married to Dr. James A. Moncure, former vice president of Elon College.

Colin King studied at the Royal College of Art, London. He started his freelance career as an illustrator, working for magazines and advertising agencies.

He began drawing pictures for children's books in 1976 and has illustrated over sixty titles to date.

Included in a wide variety of subjects are a best-selling children's encyclopedia and books about spies and detectives.

His books have been translated into several languages, including Japanese and Hebrew. He has four grown-up children and lives in Suffolk, England, with his wife, three dogs, and a cat.

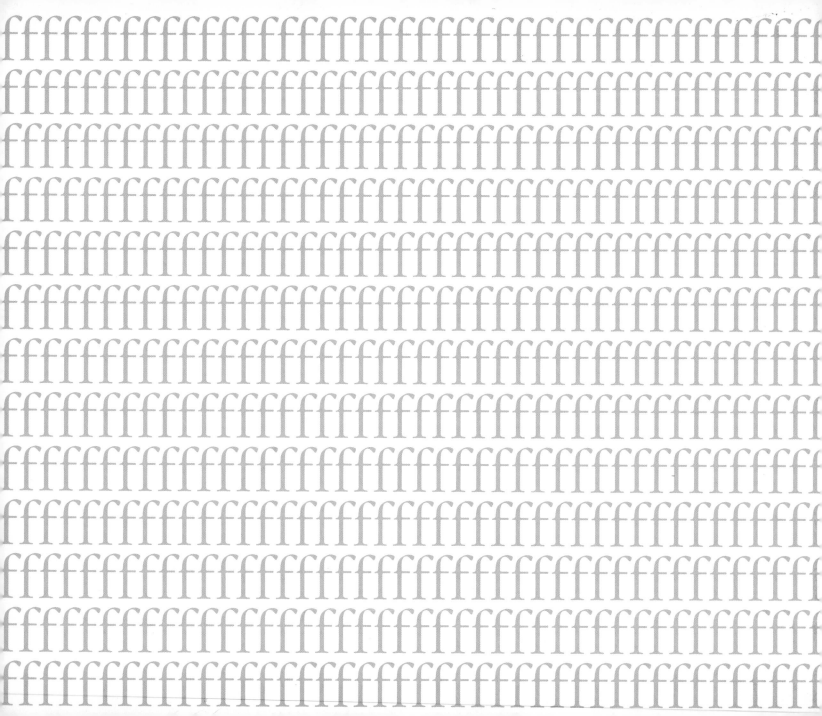